NIBBLES

For Book monsters everywhere...

... AND for ALEX, CHRIS, DANutia,
NICKy & GIDEon (who grew alongside
the BOOK). THANk you for all YOUR
LOVE and LOFTY support

EY

LITTLE TIGER PRESS LTD,
an imprint of the Little Tiger Group
1 Coda Studios, 189 Munster Road, London SW6 6AW
Imported into the EEA by Penguin Random House Ireland,
Morrison Chambers, 32 Nassau Street, Dublin D02 YH68
www.littletiger.co.uk

First published in Great Britain 2017
This edition published 2018
Text and illustrations copyright © Emma Yarlett 2017

ISBN 978-1-84869-692-1 • Printed in China • LTP/1800/4296/0821
10 9 8 7 6 5 4

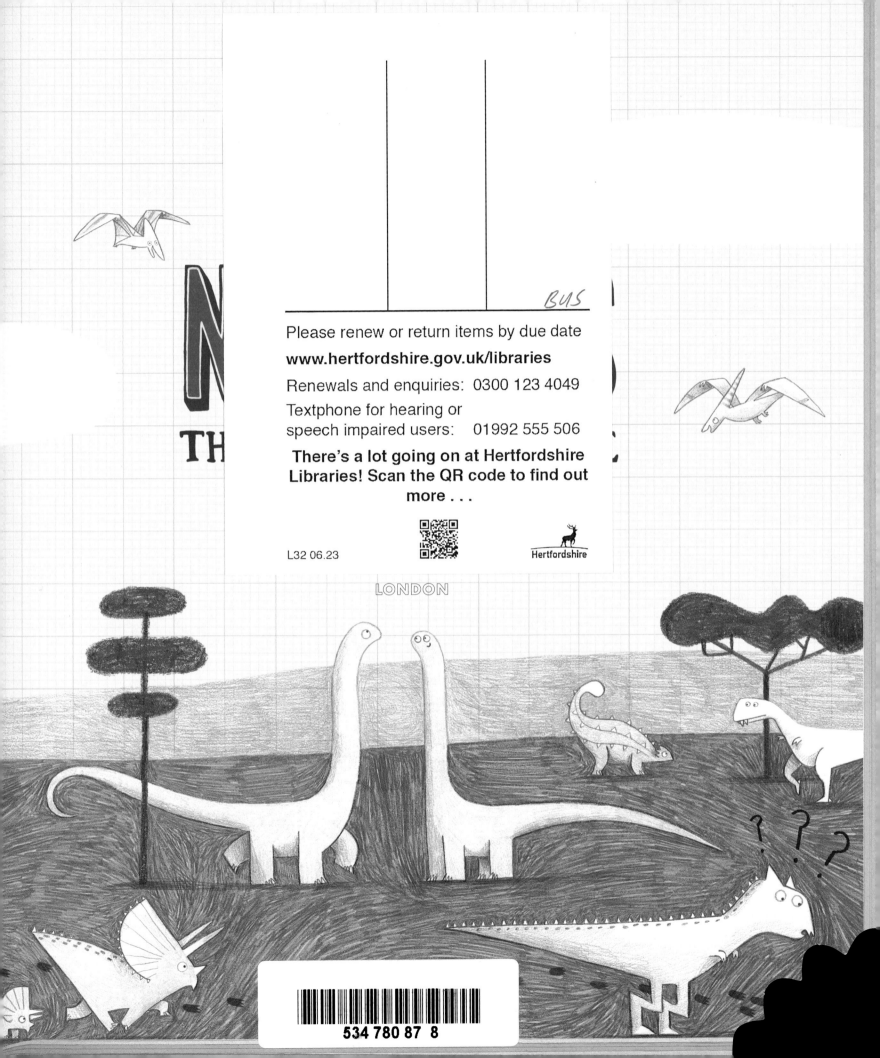

LONDON

Millions of years ago dinosaurs ruled the Earth.
In the pages of this book you will find the most
deadly, dangerous dinosaurs to ever—

WAIT A MINUTE.

WHAT IS THAT!?!

I'm trying to tell you about dinosaurs and <u>something</u> has nibbled a

GIGANTIC HOLE

in the page!

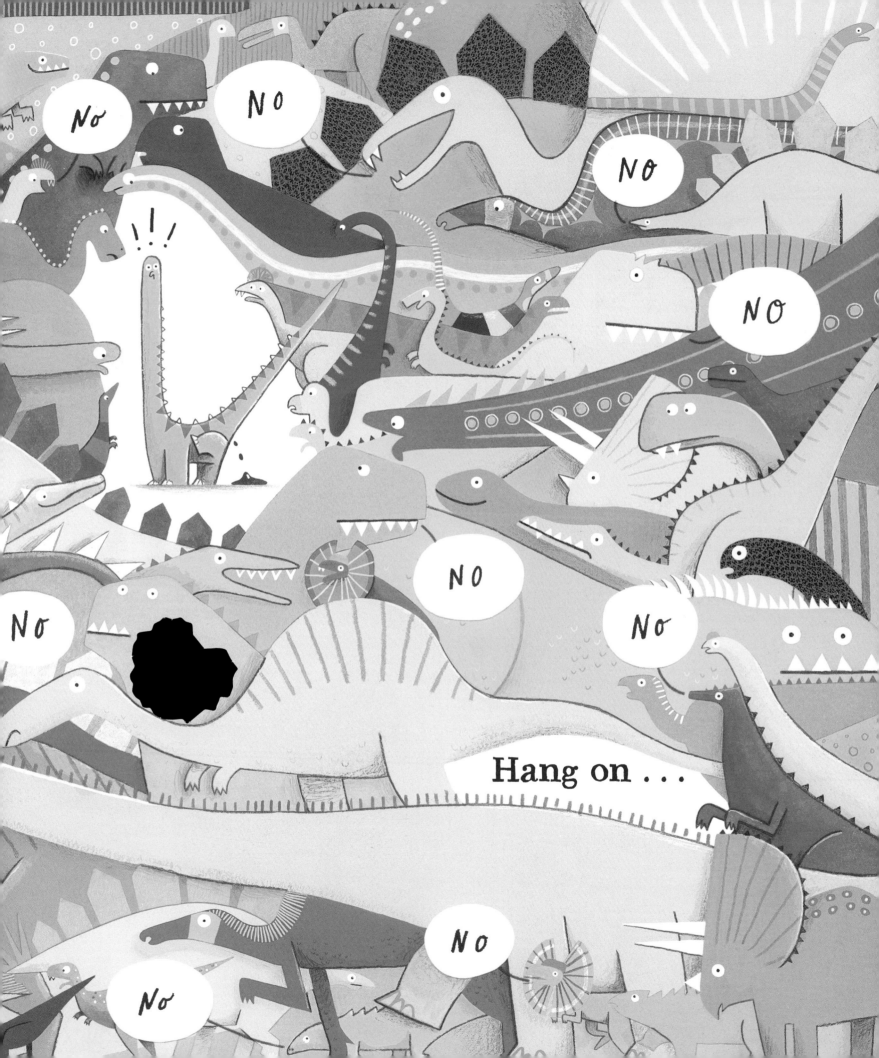

IT WAS YOU!
Who are you?
WHAT are you?

AND WHY ARE
YOU NIBBLING
THIS BOOK?!

NIBBLES

nib – ULS

Species data

Characteristics

Classification

YOU'RE NOT A DINOSAUR! You don't belong here,
it's too **DANGEROUS!** Wait! What's that noise?

NIBBLE

CHOMP

GNAW

Can you see where
Nibbles went?

Uh-oh! He's nibbled his way into the Triceratops chapter!

INTRUDER!

DAD?!?

Nibbles,
watch out!

TRICERATOPS

tri–SERRA–tops

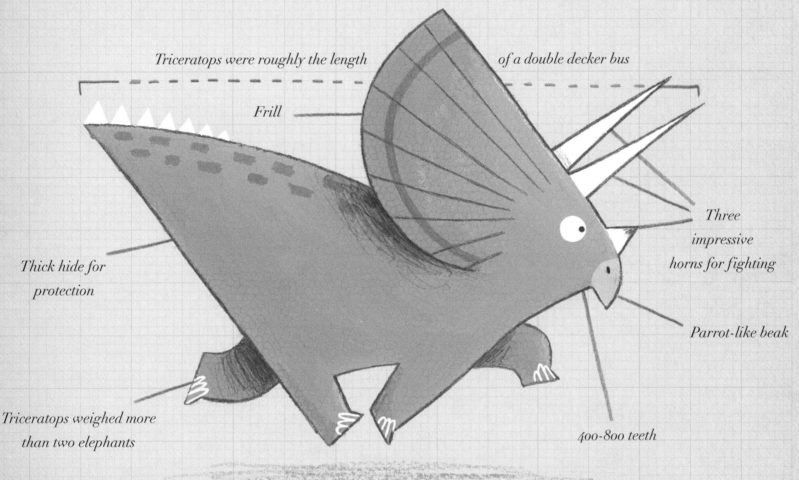

Triceratops were roughly the length of a double decker bus

Frill

Three impressive horns for fighting

Thick hide for protection

Parrot-like beak

400-800 teeth

Triceratops weighed more than two elephants

Length: 9 metres

Height: 3 metres

Weight: 6 tonnes

Diet: Herbivore

Footprint:

Triceratops had exceptionally big heads. Scientists say that they had big bums and large stompy feet too.

HA!

HOW RUDE!

LOOK! Here are ten HOT-HEADED Triceratops . . . but no Nibbles. Oh, where can he be?

CHARGE!

DIPLODOCUS

[dih–PLOD–oh–cus]

Diplodocus ate several tonnes of food every single day

Scientists used to believe that Diplodocus had a trunk

Diplodocus could outrun a human

Diplodocus was longer than — — — *a standard swimming pool*

TA!

POO!

Length: 26 metres

Height: 14 metres

Weight: 10 tonnes

Diet: Herbivore

Footprint:

A single Diplodocus fart may have contained enough GAS to fill a hot air balloon.

Did you know that a Diplodocus poop could weigh up to two tonnes and could form a ten-metre-wide poo puddle! That is nearly as wide as two cars!

CRIKEY! Here's a herd of GREEDY Diplodocus. Watch out, Nibbles! Those dippy Diplodocus might accidentally eat YOU!

HEY! WHO'S THIS?
WOW! He can eat A LOT for a little guy!
NOT as much as ME!
Let the EATING CONTEST BEGIN!

ALAN, why?!!?
I'm the PRINCE of PARPS!
GOODNESS ME! That was a WHOPPER!
PARRR
There goes NIBBLES!
OH my!

VELOCIRAPTOR

[Vel–OS–ih–RAP–tor]

Velociraptors had feathers but it's unlikely that they could fly

A big and intelligent brain

Velociraptors had a bite as powerful as a lion's

Strong legs with a top speed of 24 mph

Velociraptors were about as tall as a koala bear

Length: 2 metres

Height: 0.6 metres

Weight: 15 kgs

Diet: Carnivore

Footprints:

CATCH that NAUGHTY NIBBLER!

swift clever raptors were also thieves. Their brains were large for their puny heads. They had a terrifying temper too.

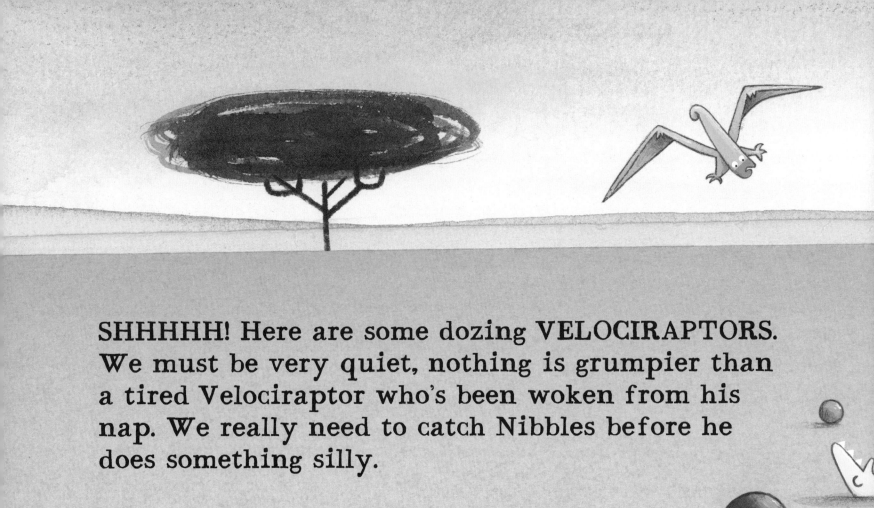

SHHHHH! Here are some dozing VELOCIRAPTORS. We must be very quiet, nothing is grumpier than a tired Velociraptor who's been woken from his nap. We really need to catch Nibbles before he does something silly.

Too late. Quick, Nibbles, hide!

TYRANNOSAURUS REX

[ti—RAN—oh—SORE—us—REX]

A large intelligent brain

Incredible sense of smell

Some of the biggest teeth ever known

Strong tail for balance and agility

Powerful legs, perfect for running, jumping and climbing

Tyrannosaurus rex was almost as long as three cars

Tyrannosaurus rex translates from the Greek (*tyrannos* / TYRANT) and Latin (*rex* / KING) to mean TYRANT LIZARD KING!

Length: 12 metres
Height: 5 metres
Weight: 7 tonnes
Diet: Carnivore
Footprint:

RUN, Nibbles!
RUN! You're
about to be . . .

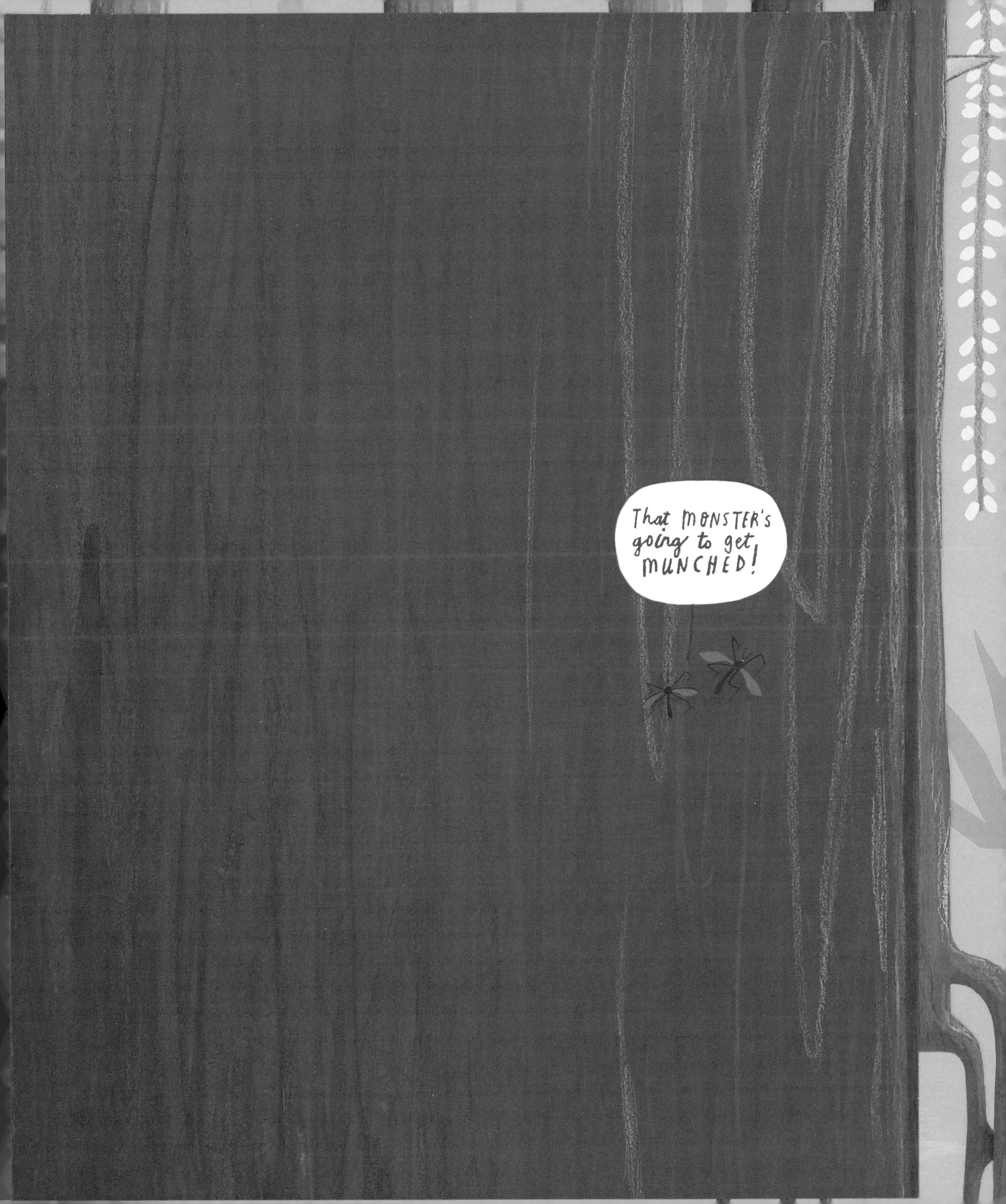
That MONSTER's going to get MUNCHED!

HOORAY! T.rex has spat him right out of the book! Bye-bye, Nibbles! Be careful what you nibble into next.